FOR ALISON LOWE
WITH LOVE
~C.P.

FOR JULIA AND VICKY
WITH LOVE
~J.C.

First published in the United States 1998 by
Little Tiger Press,
N16 W23390 Stoneridge Drive, Waukesha, WI 53188
Originally published in Great Britain 1998 by
Magi Publications, London
Text © 1998 Caroline Pitcher
Illustrations © 1998 Jane Chapman
All rights reserved.
Library of Congress Cataloging-in-Publication Data
Pitcher, Caroline,
Run with the wind / by Caroline Pitcher;
illustrated by Jane Chapman.
p.   cm.
Summary : A mother horse reassures her young foal that soon
he will be big enough to stay by himself and not even miss her.
ISBN 1-888444-29-0 (hc)
[1. Horses—Fiction. 2. Mother and child—Fiction.
3. Growth—Fiction.]
I. Chapman, Jane, 1970- ill. II. Title.
PZ7. P6427Yo 1998 [E]—DC21 97-29406 CIP AC
Printed in Italy
First American Edition
1 3 5 7 9 10 8 6 4 2

Run
with the
Wind

BY CAROLINE PITCHER

PICTURES BY JANE CHAPMAN

One moonlit night, while the wind raged and
the rain drummed on the stable roof, a foal was born.
His mother the mare breathed on him softly until he
struggled up on a tangle of long legs.

"What's that noise?" asked the foal.

"Just the wind," answered the mare, nuzzling his velvety neck.

"Where is the wind?"

"It's blowing in the hills," replied his mother. "When you are big and your legs aren't wobbly anymore, you will run with the wind over the hills."

"Will you be there with me?" asked the foal.

"No," said his mother. "But you won't think of me then."

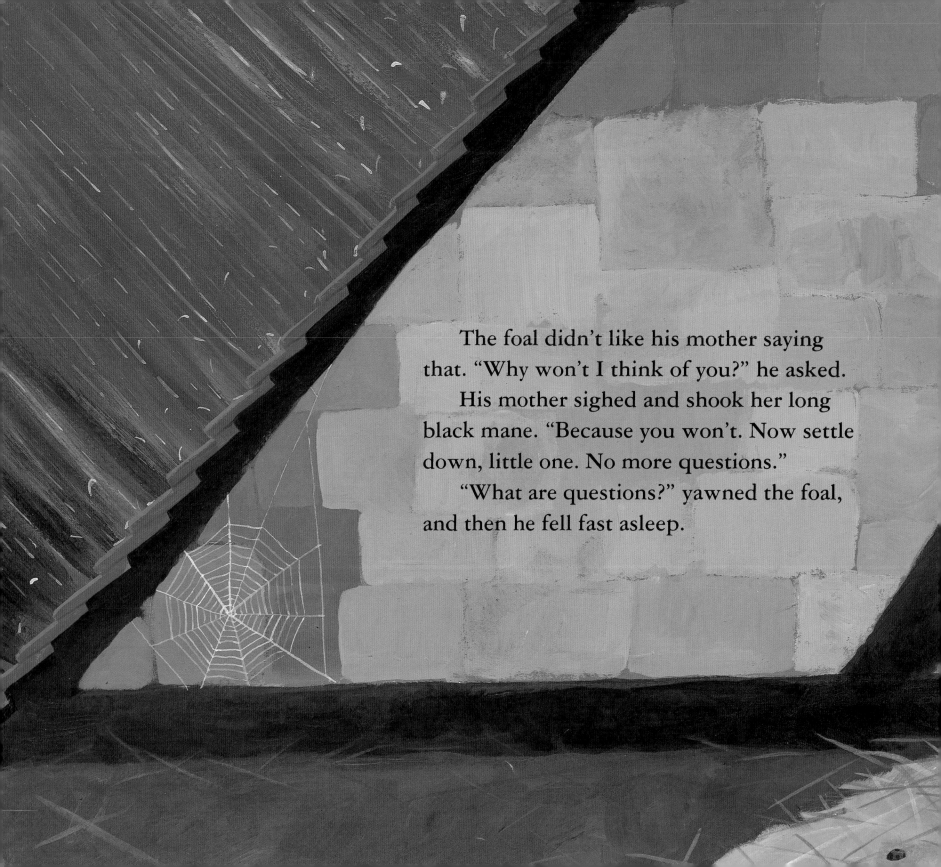

The foal didn't like his mother saying
that. "Why won't I think of you?" he asked.
His mother sighed and shook her long
black mane. "Because you won't. Now settle
down, little one. No more questions."
"What are questions?" yawned the foal,
and then he fell fast asleep.

Spring came, and the foal's legs
grew longer and stronger so that his
head just reached the top of the stable
door. "What's outside?" he asked.

"It's a field," said the mare. "Soon
you will be able to go there with me
and run all the way around and back
again."

"I don't think I want to," said
the foal, drawing back. "I don't like
Outside. I like it here."

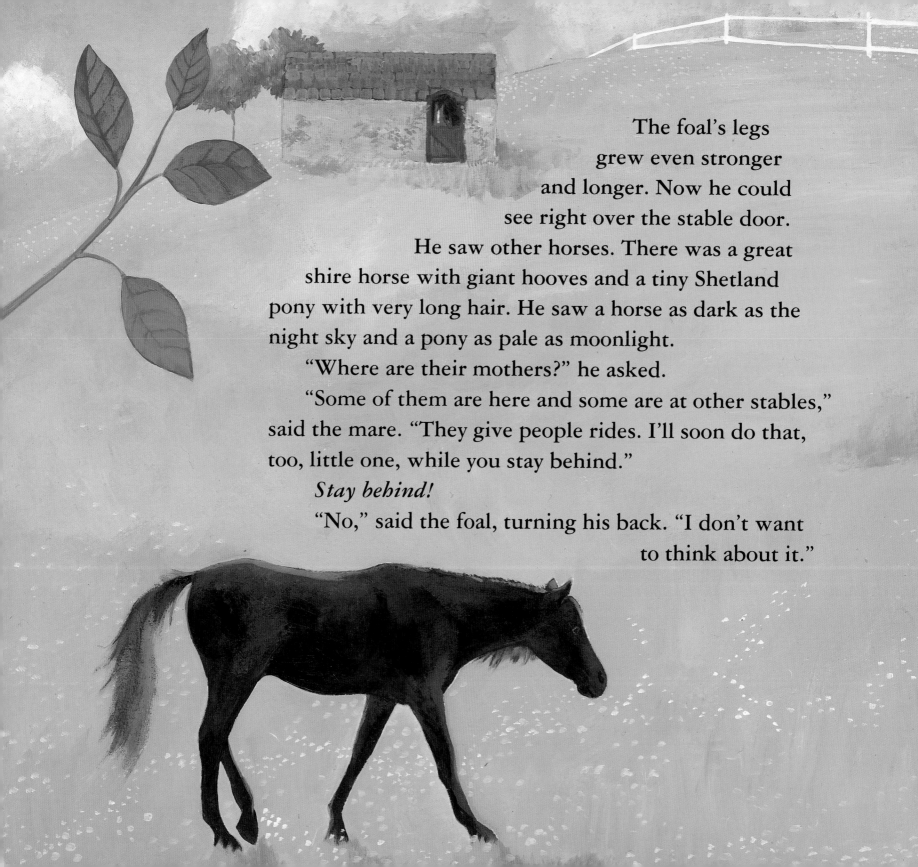

The foal's legs
grew even stronger
and longer. Now he could
see right over the stable door.
He saw other horses. There was a great
shire horse with giant hooves and a tiny Shetland
pony with very long hair. He saw a horse as dark as the
night sky and a pony as pale as moonlight.

"Where are their mothers?" he asked.

"Some of them are here and some are at other stables,"
said the mare. "They give people rides. I'll soon do that,
too, little one, while you stay behind."

Stay behind!

"No," said the foal, turning his back. "I don't want
to think about it."

When the days grew warmer,
the mare and her foal went out
into the field. They ran all the way
around it and back again.

Twilight fell, and the foal became uneasy.

"Can't we go back to the stable now?" he asked.

"No," said his mother. "When the nights are warm, we stay outside."

"But it's *dark!*"

"It's dark in the stable, too, little one. It's the same dark."

"It's not such a big dark there," said the foal. "I can't see you out here when you move away from me. I'm all alone."

"You know I'm here, even if you can't see me," whispered the mare.

The foal lifted his head in the darkness.
"What's making that noise?" he asked.

"Just the wind. Don't you remember
hearing it when you were very small?"

"Yes," said the foal. "But where is it?"

"You know it's there, but you can't see it."

"Just like you in the dark, Mom," he
whispered.

One morning, the foal woke late.
He had done so much running and
growing the day before he was very tired.
But where was his mother?

The foal looked inside the stable, but
she wasn't there. Then he saw her by the
fence. She had a bridle on her head and
a saddle on her back.

"I'm going to work," she called to
him. "I'm going to give rides again."

"And who will ride me?"
cried the foal with excitement.

"You're too little to be ridden
yet," explained his mother.

"Your back is weak, your
mouth is soft as silk,
and your legs would
snap like twigs."

"But I'll be all alone,"
he wailed. "Oh, please
stay with me!"

"No," said the mare as a little girl climbed
onto her back. "You'll be just fine."

The foal watched as his mother and her
rider trotted out of sight. He was all alone.

"Come back, Mom!" he neighed, and his
voice echoed in the hills.

He heard something answer him, but it wasn't his mother. It was the wind! The wind had come down from the hills to play with him. It blew in his mane and his tail, and it blew in the trees and stirred all the leaves. It blew a butterfly for the foal to chase, and it blew a path in the meadow that he could run right through. It even blew waves in the water of his drinking trough.

The foal jumped and ran and bucked and chased and flicked his little black tail. He ran with the wind all morning.

And then, just as the foal was too tired to run and jump anymore, his mother came back. She nuzzled his neck and said, "You see—nothing bad happened to you when you were alone."

Oh my, thought the foal. I was having so much fun I didn't think of her once.

"I wasn't alone," he said. "The wind played with me."

"So you didn't think of me at all?"

"Well, maybe a *little* bit," said the foal.

"That's good," said the mare. "I was thinking of you the whole time!"